NAILED IT!

Extreme STREET LUGING

Virginia Loh-Hagan

45th Parallel Press

Published in the United States of America by Cherry Lake Publishing
Ann Arbor, Michigan
www.cherrylakepublishing.com

Content Adviser: Liv Williams, Editor, www.iLivExtreme.com
Reading Adviser: Marla Conn, ReadAbility, Inc.
Photo Credits: ©Explorer Media Pty Ltd Sport The Library/Dreamstime.com, cover, 1; ©Purestock/Thinkstock.com, 5; ©David Crockett/Shutterstock.com, 6; ©Duomo/Corbis, 8; ©Buzz Pictures/Alamy Stock Photo, 11; ©Buzz Picture /Alamy Stock Photo 12; ©Buzz Pictures Alamy Stock Photo, 15; ©Buzz Pictures/Alamy Stock Photo, 17; ©Buzz Pictures/Alamy Stock Photo, 19; ©Lucidwaters/Dreamstime.com, 21; ©Colleen Cleveland/www.colleencleveland.com, 23; ©Colleen Cleveland/www.colleencleveland.com, 24; ©David Crockett/Shutterstock.com, 27; ©Cheng Jiang/ZUMA Press/Newscom, 28; ©Trusjom/Shutterstock.com, multiple interior pages; ©Kues/Shutterstock.com, multiple interior pages

45th Parallel Press is an imprint of Cherry Lake Publishing.

Library of Congress Cataloging-in-Publication Data

Loh-Hagan, Virginia.
Extreme street luging / by Virginia Loh-Hagan .
pages cm. -- (Nailed it!)
Includes bibliographical references and index.
ISBN 978-1-63470-488-5 (hardcover) -- ISBN 978-1-63470-548-6 (pdf) -- ISBN 978-1-63470-608-7 (paperback) -- ISBN 978-1-63470-668-1 (ebook)
1. Street luge racing--Juvenile literature. 2. Extreme sports--Juvenile literature. I. Title.
GV859.82.L65 2016
796.6'7--dc23
2015026816

ABOUT THE AUTHOR

Dr. Virginia Loh-Hagan is an author, university professor, former classroom teacher, and curriculum designer. She prefers walking downhill slowly. She lives in San Diego with her very tall husband and very naughty dogs. To learn more about her, visit www.virginialoh.com.

Table of Contents

1

Speed Kings and Queens

Who is Tom Mason? Who is Erik Shafer? Who is David Dean? Who is Pamela Zoolalian? What are gravity sports?

Tom Mason is on his back. He's on a board. He's 1 inch (2.5 centimeters) off the ground. He races downhill. He turns tight corners. He hopes no cars or people are in his path.

Mason is "The Bad Boy of Street Luge." He's the fastest street luger in the world. He went 81.28 miles (131 kilometers) per hour. He said, "For a few seconds, I am truly flying like Superman and feel like a speeding bullet."

He started street luging at night. There was no traffic. His first race day was surprising. He had never luged during the day. He was scared. He saw telephone poles, fences, and cliffs. He overcame his fear.

Erik Shafer raced against others. He crashed into them. Others crashed into him. He cracked two ribs. He tore arm muscles. He loves speed.

Street luging can be aggressive. This is when people play rough.

There are lots of high-speed crashes in street luging.

David Dean started competing at age 14. In one race, he was the first person to go downhill. He crashed halfway. He broke his hand.

He competed the next year. Someone crashed in front of him. He broke both legs. He kept racing. He got better and better.

He said, "To be able to play in the road and go as fast as you want and go nuts is cool."

Pamela Zoolalian raced downhill. She made sharp turns. She spun out of control. She flipped in the air. She hurt her shoulder.

NAILED IT!

Spotlight Biography: Beagle Jarvis

William "Beagle" Jarvis helped develop street luging. He said, "I don't want it to be seen as an alternative sport. I want to be a mainstream athlete." He wants street luging to be more popular. He grew up in Madison County. It's in New York. He started with skateboarding. Then, he lay down on the board. He went faster. He liked street luging better. Once, he almost crashed into a milk truck. He street luged down a hill. The truck came around the corner. He was going 60 miles (96.5 km) per hour. He couldn't stop. He went under the truck. He came out the other side. He said, "Luge is great. I love it." He organizes contests for street lugers in his hometown. It's called the Madison County Gravity Fest. It's his way of giving back to the sport.

The Gravity Games was a big sports competition. It was like the X-Games.

She fell hard. But she got up quickly. She said, "I think that's what gave me the level of respect that I've gotten. Because the guys see me just take the hardest knocks, get up, shake it off, and go again."

She's a speed queen. She's one of the few females doing street luging. She's the only female who competed in the sport at the Gravity Games. These games focused on **gravity sports**. Athletes use gravity to push them forward and downhill.

"She's a speed queen."

2

Gravity-Powered Sport

What is street luging? What are street luging races? What are street luging boards? What is street luging gear?

Street luging is a gravity sport. It doesn't use **motors**. A motor is a machine that provides power. Street luging gets power from going downhill.

Street luge races are intense. Up to six athletes compete. They bump each other. They pass each other. The first one to cross the finish line wins. They race on mountain roads. They race on city roads.

Not everyone competes in races. Many do it for fun. They race down roads. They race down tracks. They race down hills.

Smooth roads lead to faster rides. High slopes create more force and speed. Lugers can go more than 80 miles (129 km) per hour.

They lie down on **modified** skateboards. Modified means changed or customized. Street luging boards look like wheeled sleds. It's the only thing separating lugers from the street. They can feel the high speeds. They can feel bumps.

Street luging is also known as land luging or road luging.

A street luging board is sometimes called a sled.

Street lugers are called **pilots**. They steer by changing their weight. They **navigate**, or find their way. They sit in a **supine** position. This means they're lying faceup. Their backs are flat on the boards. This means there's little wind resistance. They can go faster.

They can increase their speed with their bodies. They point their toes. They keep their heads down. They keep their bodies flat.

Pilots put their feet on pegs. They can steer with their feet. They lift their heads a little to see.

NAILED IT!

Advice from the Field: Abdil Mahdzan

Abdil Mahdzan is from Malaysia. He's a World Cup champion in street luge. He built his own luge. He started racing when he was in college. He's competed in six continents. He likes to ride fast. His best speed is 81.4 miles (131 km) per hour. He likes challenging roads. He likes street luging on new terrains. Terrain refers to land and its physical features. He advises pilots to respect others. He said, "Staying in your own lane is common sense, not just for your own safety, but also for the reputation of our sport. We do not want to be perceived by motorists as reckless, dangerous individuals seeking a death wish." He wants people to know pilots are real athletes. He stays in his own lane. He thinks ahead. He thinks about what oncoming cars could do. He remains alert. He's a problem solver.

Boards do not have brakes. Pilots brake with their feet. They put their feet on the ground. They drag them. This slows down the boards. They can stop. They wear special shoes. The shoes are made of leather or rubber. Some pilots even add pieces of tire to their shoes.

They wear helmets. Helmets have full face masks. They protect the head. They wear gloves to protect their hands. They wear **leathers**. Leathers are racing suits. They're made of leather.

Gloves have rubber pads on the fingers to help lugers push off.

3

Street Danger

What are the dangers of street luging? How do pilots reduce their risks? How is street luging against the law?

Any sport with high speeds is dangerous. Helmets and suits are pilots' only protection. Leather protects skin. But sometimes pilots go too fast. They drag their leather shoes, gloves, and suits. It's like a match striking the surface. Leather can burn. It can smoke. It can catch fire.

Pilots try to keep their wheels on the ground. But sometimes they can't. They're going too fast. They can end up in the air. They can flip over. They fall. They get bumps and bruises. They get broken bones. They get head injuries.

Pilots can't make mistakes. They can't lose control. They could crash into others. They could crash into hay. Bundles of hay mark the sides of the racetracks. The hay also protects fans. Pilots could crash into fans or objects.

Street lugers can get road rash. Road rash is scrapes and cuts.

NAILED IT!

That Happened?!?

Skyline Rotorua is in New Zealand. It's like an amusement park. It built the first luge track. Skyline Luge is a popular gravity ride. The luge combines a go-kart and a sled. It has three wheels. It has seats. It has handlebars. Riders have full control over speed and direction. They pull back handlebars to slow down or stop. They push handlebars forward to go forward. The track is downhill. It's the longest track of its kind. It has turns. It has twists. It has tunnels. Riders can go 300 miles (483 km) per hour. Some people say it's the closest thing to real-life Mario Kart games. People have gotten hurt. One man crashed into a wall. He broke his ankle. Another woman crashed. She passed out. She was flown to a hospital. She was treated for back and head injuries.

Accidents happen. An Australian woman lost control around a corner. She slammed into a rail. She died. Another woman was killed by a pilot. The pilot didn't see her. She couldn't get out of the way fast enough.

One pilot tested a new board. He rode over an uneven part of the road. He wobbled. His left foot was injured. He used his right foot to slow down. He ran off the road. He fell in the grass and rocks.

The hay bundles stand between the lugers and the fans.

Pilots try to reduce risks. They walk their course. They learn about the land. They look for holes or cracks. They look for objects. They check their gear.

In many cities, street luging is against the law. Pilots on a street luge can be considered **vehicles**. Vehicles are like cars. Pilots often go past the speed limit. They get in trouble. Street luging is like skateboarding. Skateboarding is banned in many places. A police official said, "High-risk activities like luge and public roads don't mix."

Theme parks try to make luging safer.

4 From Skateboarding to Street Luging

How did street luging develop? What other sports influenced street luging? What is the Signal Hill Speed Run? How is street luging different from ice luging?

Street luging developed in the 1970s. It developed in Southern California. Skateboarders raced down steep hills. But they wanted to go even faster. They lay down on their skateboard. This was called buttboarding.

The Signal Hill Speed Run started in 1975. It was the world's first downhill skateboard race. In 1976, Sam Puccio Jr. rode on his back. He won. Some people were upset. They thought he should be standing. But the rules let riders choose their position. In 1977, street luging became its own category in the Signal Hill Speed Run. There were many crashes. There were many injuries. By 1978, the race stopped.

Pilots kept promoting the sport. They hosted races. They improved the boards. Bob Pereyra is one of the fastest street luge pilots. He started the Road Racers Association for International Luge (RAIL). He said, "Everything I have goes directly into this sport."

Street luging was started by skateboarders.

Street lugers created organizations and compete in big contests.

Street luging developed from skateboarding. But it also developed from ice luging. Ice luging is shooting down an ice tunnel. Street luging developed in areas where there's no snow.

Street luging is different from ice luging. Street luge boards are longer. They have wheels instead of **runners**. Runners are like skating blades. Ice luge boards end at the pilot's neck. Ice lugers have to hold their heads up.

Extreme Street Luging: Know the Lingo

Bacon: a rough, uneven, or otherwise dangerous road

Banana: a luger whose luge slips out from under him

Chucking bale: crashing into hay bales, or bundles, and moving them

Drop a hill: riding a luge course, preferably a closed one

Flesh wing: when a pilot extends an arm for balance during a difficult part of the course

G-force: the force to which a body is subjected when it's accelerated

Puke a wheel: losing a wheel as a result of flames or melting

Rafting: when a pilot is forced to regain speed by pushing himself forward with his hands after an unplanned stop

Scrambled eggs: a rough stretch of road, but less rough than bacon

Sturz: crash

Wad: a multi-luge collision

Wobbs: the shaking or wobbling of the luge when reaching very high speeds

5

Faster Than Speeding Rockets

How do pilots make street luging even more extreme? Who is Billy Copeland? Who is Joel King? Who is Jason Bradbury?

Pilots look for the next extreme level. They practice rocket luging or powered-street luging. The boards are connected to motors. The motors are powered by gas or electric. This sport combines street luging and car racing.

Billy Copeland grew up in Tennessee. He didn't have big hills. He needed more power. He saw a show about rockets. He put 24 rocket boosters on his board. He set off. He wobbled. He regained control. He braked. He said, "Once I hit those rockets, I stop being a driver and become a passenger." He set records for rocket luging. First, he went 70 miles (112.6 km) per hour. Then he went 98.5 miles (158.5 km) per hour.

Joel King is a street luging champion. He attached a jet engine to his board. He broke Copeland's record. He raced 112 miles (180 km) per hour. His jet engine gave him 80 pounds (36 kilograms) of thrust.

Street lugers push the limits of speed.

Jean-Yves Blondeau takes street luging to the next level.

He failed the first time. The track was rough. There were troubles with the engine. He tried again. He went faster.

Jason Bradbury rode a jet-powered street luge. He beat King's record. He went 115.83 miles (186.4 km) per hour. He almost died on his first try. He skidded. He crashed at 100 miles (161 km) per hour.

Street luging pilots are always challenging themselves.

NAILED IT!

When Extreme Is Too Extreme!

Can you imagine street luging face-first? Jean-Yves Blondeau can. He's a French stuntman. He's known as "Rollerman." He invented a 32-wheeled roller suit. The suit uses rollerblade wheels. The wheels are placed on his joints, chest, and back. He looks like a human luge. He can ride in different positions. He can go 70 miles (112.6 km) per hour downhill. His suit has been featured in movies and television. He trained Jackie Chan to use the suit. It was for the movie Chinese Zodiac. He used the suit in China. He went more than 50 miles (80.5 km) per hour. He went down Tianmen Mountain. He went down 6.5 miles (10.5 km). He handled 99 tight corners. He did it in under 20 minutes. He uses his body to steer and fix speed. He's done several stunts. He overtakes motorcycles. He catches air. He rides roadside cliffs with no rails. He calls the new sport Buggy Rollin.

Did You Know?

- Street luging pilots go fast downhill. They experience a lot of force. It's almost the same force as jet fighter pilots face.
- Some street luging pilots wear special vests. They sew pieces of lead into the vests. Lead is really heavy. It helps make them heavier. This gives them more speed.
- Street luging was featured in *Charlie's Angels: Full Throttle*. A stuntwoman street luges down a winding highway. She moves next to a silver car. She links herself to the car. There are rocks on the road. It's a bumpy ride. The scene was nominated for Best Specialty Stunt in the Taurus World Stunt Awards.
- Malik "The Fast" Smith is the world's youngest street luging pilot. He turned nine in 2016. He competed in the National Street Luge Tour and others. Malik's dad is also a pilot.
- Vikings are believed to be the first users of sleds. They started using them in the year 800.
- Tom Mason was disqualified twice. This means he was kicked out of a contest. The judges said he caused accidents. The accidents hurt his opponents. His gold and bronze medals were taken away from him.
- It's hard to street luge when it rains. The rain makes the roads wet. It's hard to get traction. Pilots have to slow down. Otherwise, they'd fly off the roads.

Consider This!

TAKE A POSITION! Some people think street luging is safer than skateboarding. Lugers sit closer to the ground. This gives them more balance and control. Lugers have a shorter distance to fall. Other people think street luging is more dangerous than skateboarding. Lugers move at faster speeds. Lugers can only practice down hills. Which sport do you think is safer: skateboarding or street luging? Argue your point with reasons and evidence.

SAY WHAT? Street luging is inspired by skateboarding and ice luging. Explain how street luging is similar to these sports. Explain how it is different from these sports.

THINK ABOUT IT! Street luging is an alternative sport. This means it's not very well known. There is only a small population of people who practice street luging. There may not be a ton of people street luging. But it's a very strong community. What do you think it means to be a member of the street luging community?

SEE A DIFFERENT SIDE! City officials hold street lugers to the same rules as skateboarders and cars. Lugers have to stay on the right ride of the street. They need to stay under the speed limit. Why do you think city officials do this?

Learn More: Resources

PRIMARY SOURCES

"Street Luge," a video (History Channel, Modern Marvels) at www.history.com/shows/modern-marvels/videos/sports-gadgets-street-luge

SECONDARY SOURCES

Blomquist, Christopher. *Street Luge in the X Games*. New York: PowerKids Press, 2003.

Murdico, Suzanne J. *Street Luge and Dirtboarding*. New York: Rosen Central, 2003.

Orr, Tamra B. *Extreme Street Luge*. New York: Marshall Cavendish Benchmark, 2012.

WEB SITES

International Downhill Federation: www.internationaldownhillfederation.org

International Gravity Sports Association: www.igsaworldcup.com

World Gravity Speed Association: http://wgsa.weebly.com/streetluge.html

Glossary

gravity sports (GRAV-ih-tee SPORTS) games in which athletes use gravity to push them forward

leathers (LETH-urz) street luging racing suits that are made of leather

modified (MAH-duh-fyed) changed or customized

motors (MOH-turz) machines that provide power

navigate (NAV-ih-gate) to find a way

pilots (PYE-luhts) preferred term for street luger, someone who does street luging

runners (RUHN-urz) blades on ice luge sleds or ice skates

supine (soo-PINE) lying down

vehicles (VEE-ih-kuhlz) things on wheels, like cars and trucks, that are used to transport people or goods

Index